HIGGLETY PIGGLETY POP!

233 Playful Rhymes and Chants for your Baby

BY "MISS JACKIE" WEISSMAN

© 1991 by Jackie Weissman

ISBN 0-939514-29-X

Published by:

Miss Jackie Music Co.
10001 El Monte
Overland Park, Kansas 66207

Printed in the United States of America.

Cover design and illustrations by Diane Foster

Distributed by:

Gryphon House
3706 Otis Street
P.O. Box 211
Mt. Ranier, Maryland 20822

FROM THE AUTHOR

Children develop language through imitating rhythmic patterns. Rhymes and chants are the perfect vehicle for language development, shared fun and bonding.

Many of the rhymes and chants in this book are mine or adaptations of traditional literature. I have made every effort to identify the original sources.

For the past 12 years, I have met with parents and babies in intimate groups to share music, movement, games, fun, loving and bonding. The parents have shared with me many rhymes and chants that they sing and say with their babies.

I hope you enjoy these rhymes and chants as much as I have enjoyed researching and writing them.

--Jackie Weissman

TABLE OF CONTENTS

WAKING UP

Diaper Time

It's diaper time,
It's diaper time,
This is baby's favorite time.
One, two, three, four,
Take the diaper off!

It's diaper time,
It's diaper time,
This is baby's favorite time.
One, two, three, four,
Put the diaper on!

Acka Backa

Acka backa, soda cracker,
Acka backa boo.
(While baby is in her crib, gently swing her arms.)
Acka backa soda cracker,
I love you.
(Pick up the baby and cuddle her.)

Acka backa, soda cracker,
Acka backa boo.
Acka backa soda cracker,
Up goes you!
(Hold the baby high in the air.)

WAKING UP

Little Boy Blue

Little Boy Blue,
Come blow your horn,
The sheep's in the meadow,
The cow's in the corn.
Where is the boy
Who looks after the sheep?
He's under the haystack
Fast asleep.
Will you wake him?
No, not I!
For if I do,
He's sure to cry.
Wake up, wake up, wake up!

Tippety Tin

Tippety, tippety, tippety, tin,
Give me a kiss, and I'll come in.
Tippety, tippety, tippety, toe,
Give me a kiss, and I will go.

Tippety, tippety, tippety, tin,
Give me a pancake, and I'll come in.
Tippety, tippety, tippety, toe,
Give me a pancake and I will go.

WAKING UP

Little Train

The little train ran up the track,
Toot, toot, toot.
The little train ran up the track
And then it came toot- tooting back.
(Run your fingers up and down the baby's arms.)

Good Morning Toes

Good morning toes,
And how are you today?
I trust you had a good night's sleep
And are ready now to play.
(Wiggle the baby's toe.)

Good morning knees,
And how are you today?
I trust you had a good night's sleep,
And are ready now to play.
(Wiggle the baby's knee.)

Repeat the rhyme substituting other body parts.

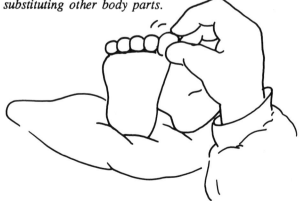

WAKING UP

What the Baby Says

Tell me, what the baby says,
Ma ma, ma ma.
Tell me, what the baby says,
Ma, ma ma.

Tell me, what the clock says,
Tick tock, tick tock.
Tell me, what the clock says,
Tick, tick tock.

Tell me, what the birdie says,
Tweet, tweet, tweet, tweet.
Tell me, what the birdie says,
Tweet, tweet, tweet.

Tell me, what the drum says...
Tell me, what the water says...
Tell me, what the horn says...

Baby's Eyes

Where are the baby's eyes?
Here are the baby's eyes.
(Touch the baby's eyes.)
Pretty eyes, pretty eyes,
I love you.

Where's the baby's nose?
Here's the baby's nose.
(Touch the baby's nose.)
Pretty nose, pretty nose,
I love you.

Where's the baby's cheek?
Here's the baby's cheek.
(Touch the baby's cheek.)
Pretty cheek, pretty cheek,
I love you.

WAKING UP

Creeping

Creeping, creeping, creeping,
(Creep fingers up the baby's arm.)
Comes the little cat.
Meow, meow, meow, meow,
Meow, meow, meow, meow,
Just like that.

Creeping, creeping, creeping,
Comes the little bunny.
Hop, hop, hop, hop,
Hop, hop, hop, hop,
Do you think that's funny?

This Little Boy

This little boy
Is going to bed,
Down on the pillow,
He lays his head.
Morning comes,
He opens his eyes,
Off with a toss,
The covers flies.
Soon he is dressed
And out to play,
Ready for fun,
All the day.

WAKING UP

Porridge Is Bubbling

Porridge is bubbling,
Bubbling hot.
Stir it round,
And round in the pot.

The bubbles plip,
The bubbles plop,
It's ready to eat,
All bubbling hot.

Wake up baby,
Wake up soon.
We'll eat the porridge,
With a spoon.

Ride a Cock Horse

Ride a cock horse to Banbury Cross,
To see a fine lady on a white horse.
(Bounce the baby on your knee.)
Rings on her fingers and bells on her toes,
She shall have music wherever she goes.

Ride a cock horse to Banbury Cross,
To see what Tommy can buy,
A penny white loaf,
A penny white cake,
And a two penny apple pie.

WAKING UP

A Walk One Day

When I went out for a walk one day,
My head fell off and rolled away.
And when I saw that it was gone,
I picked it up and put it on.

When I went into the street,
Someone shouted, "Look at your feet!"
I looked at them and sadly said,
"I've left them both asleep in bed."

Red Dress

Baby's wearing a red dress,
Red dress, red dress.
Baby's wearing a red dress,
All day long.

Baby's wearing a blue shirt,
Blue shirt, blue shirt.
Baby's wearing a blue shirt,
All day long.

Baby's wearing white shoes,
White shoes, white shoes.
Baby's wearing white shoes,
All day long.
*(Substitute the baby's name and sing
about the baby's clothes.)*

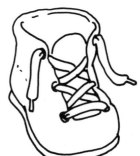

WAKING UP

Every Morning

Every morning at eight o'clock,
You can hear the milkperson,
Knock, knock, knock.
Up jumps baby to open the door,
One carton, two cartons,
Three cartons, four.

Every morning at nine o'clock,
You can hear the mail carrier
Knock, knock, knock.
Up jumps baby to open the door,
One letter, two letters,
Three letters, four.

Every morning at ten o'clock,
You can hear daddy,
Knock, knock, knock.
Up jumps baby to open the door,
One kiss, two kisses,
Three kisses, four.

Oh, Aunt Jemima

Oh, Aunt Jemima, look at your uncle Jim,
Down at the duckpond, learning how to swim.
First he does the breast stroke,
(Pretend to do the breast stroke.)
Then he does the side,
(Pretend to do the side stroke.)
Now he's under the water,
Swimming against the tide.

WAKING UP

Merry Sunshine

Good morning, merry sunshine,
How did you wake so soon?
You've scared the little stars away,
And shined away the moon.
I saw you go to sleep last night
Before I stopped my playing.
How did you get 'way over there?
And where have you been staying?

I never go to sleep, dear one,
I just go round to see
My little children of the East
Who rise and watch for me.
I waken all the birds and bees,
And flowers on my way,
And now come back to see the child,
Who stayed out late to play.

Pinkety Pinkety

Pinkety, pinkety, thumb to thumb,
Wish a wish and it's sure to come.
(Put your thumbs on the baby's thumbs.)
If yours come true, mine will come true,
(Wrap your thumbs around the baby's thumbs.)
Pinkety, pinkety, thumb to thumb.
(Kiss the baby's thumbs.)

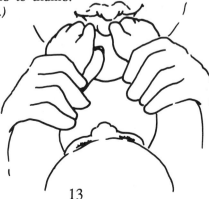

WAKING UP

Eat Brown Bread

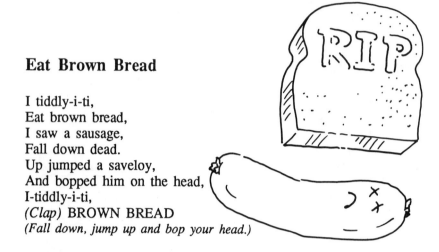

I tiddly-i-ti,
Eat brown bread,
I saw a sausage,
Fall down dead.
Up jumped a saveloy,
And bopped him on the head,
I-tiddly-i-ti,
(Clap) BROWN BREAD
(Fall down, jump up and bop your head.)

Miss Mary Mac

Miss Mary Mac, Mac, Mac
All dressed in black, black, black.
With silver buttons, buttons, buttons
All down her back, back back.

She asked her mother, mother, mother
For fifty cents, cents, cents.
To see the elephants, elephants, elephants
Jump the fence, fence, fence.

They jumped so high, high, high
They reached the sky, sky, sky.
And they didn't come back, back, back
Till the fourth of July, -ly, -ly.
(Clap the baby's hands to the rhythm.)

WAKING UP

The Wild Oak Tree

Love grows under the wild oak tree,
Sugar melts like candy,
Top of the mountain shines like gold,
And you kiss your little baby sorta handy.
(Lift your baby out of bed and rock her.)

Dreams, dreams, sweet dreams,
Under the wild oak tree,
Dreams, dreams, sweet dreams,
One for you and one for me.
(Rock the baby.)

Jump out of Bed

I jump out of bed in the morning,
I jump out of bed in the morning,
I jump out of bed in the morning,
Because it's a very nice day.

I jump out of bed and wash myself
In the morning,
I jump out of bed and wash myself,
In the morning,
I jump out of bed and wash myself,
In the morning,
Because it's a very nice day.

I dress myself in the morning.

I comb my hair in the morning.

(Repeat the verse adding new actions.)

WAKING UP

Little Tommy Tittlemouse

Little Tommy Tittlemouse
Lives in a little house.
Someone's knocking,
*(Knock gently on
the baby's forehead.)*
Me, oh, my,
Someone's calling,
It is I.
(Whisper in the baby's ear.)
It is I.
It is I.

Hickory Dickory Dock

Hickory dickory dock,
The mouse ran up the clock,
(Creep your fingers up the baby's leg.)
He took his shoes and put them on,
Hickory dickory dock.

Hickory dickory dock,
The mouse ran up the clock,
(Creep your fingers on the baby's toes.)
He took his socks and put them on,
Hickory dickory dock.

*(Repeat the rhyme substituting other
articles of clothing.)*

WAKING UP

Okki Tokki Unga

Okki tokki unga,
Okki tokki unga,
(Sway the baby's arms back and forth.)
Hey, missa day, missa doh, missa day.
(Swing the baby's arms up and down.)
Okki tokki unga,
Okki tokki unga,
Hey, missa day, missa doh, missa day.
(Repeat the same actions.)

Baby Mice

Where are the baby mice?
Squeak, squeak, squeak.
(Hide your hand behind your back.)
I cannot see them,
Peek, peek, peek.
(Bring your fist forward.)
Here they come, out of their hole,
One, two, three, four, five,
And that is all.
(Open your fist one finger at a time.)

DRESSING AND BATHTIME

Here Is the Sea

Here is the sea
The wavy sea.
(Wave your hands from side to side.)
Here is my boat
(Cup your hands like a boat.)
And here is me.
(Point to yourself.)
All of the fishes
(Wiggle all of your fingers.)
Down below.
(Point downward.)
Wiggle their tails
(Wiggle all of your fingers.)
And away they go.
(Wiggle your fingers behind your back.)

The Little Green Frog

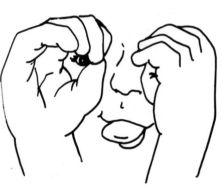

Gunk, gunk,
Went the little green frog one day.
Gunk, gunk,
Went the little green frog.
Gunk, gunk,
Went the little green frog one day.
And his eyes went ahh, ahh,
GUNK!
(Circle your fingers around your eyes and stick out your tongue.)

DRESSING AND BATHTIME

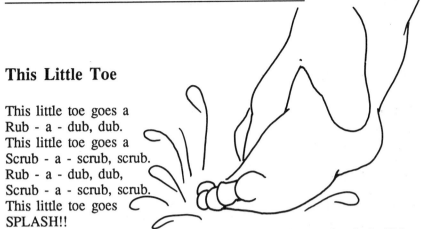

This Little Toe

This little toe goes a
Rub - a - dub, dub.
This little toe goes a
Scrub - a - scrub, scrub.
Rub - a - dub, dub,
Scrub - a - scrub, scrub.
This little toe goes
SPLASH!!
(Rub each of the baby's toes gently as you say the rhyme. Say "splash" in a silly voice.)

Charlie Chaplin

Charlie Chaplin went to France,
To teach the ladies how to dance.
First he did the rhumba,
(Move the baby's knees back and forth.)
Then he did the kicks,
(Take the baby's legs and move them in a kicking motion.)
Then he did the samba,
(Put the baby's legs together and move them up and down.)
Then he did the splits.
(Pull the baby's legs apart and then move them together.)

DRESSING AND BATHTIME

Bubbles Bubbles

Bubbles, bubbles,
Everywhere,
Floating, popping,
In the air.
(*Blow bubbles with
a bubble pipe.*)
Look through them,
Grab them quickly
Before they disappear.

Big bubbles, little bubbles,
All around the room,
Some float up and others go
BOOOOOOOOM!

Piggle Wiggle

Piggle, wiggle, piggle, wiggle,
Piggle, wiggle, say.
We always put our clothes on,
Every single day.

Piggle, wiggle, piggle, wiggle,
Piggle, wiggle, say.
We always put our shoes on,
Every single day.
(*Repeat the rhyme substituting different articles of clothing.*)

DRESSING AND BATHTIME

Wash Those Dirty Hands

Wash those dirty hands, oh,
Wash those dirty hands.
Get those fingers nice and clean,
Wash those dirty hands.
(Say in a sing-songy voice as you wash.)

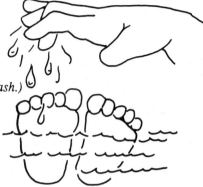

Wash those dirty feet, oh,
Wash those dirty feet.
Get those toesies nice and clean,
Wash those dirty feet.
*(As you wash, repeat the verse,
substituting different body parts.)*

Swim Little Fishie

Swim little fishie,
Swim around the pool,
(Move your hands in the water like a fish.)
Swim little fishie,
The water is cool.
(Keep moving your hands like a fish.)
Where's the little fishie?
Where did he go?
*(Put your hand
under the water.)*
There he is!
*(Stick your finger
out of the water.)*
SPLASH !!!

DRESSING AND BATHTIME

When Ducks Get up in the Morning

When ducks get up in the morning,
They always say, "Quack, quack."
When ducks get up in the morning,
They always say, "Quack, quack."
Quack, quack, quack,
Quack, quack, quack,
They always say, "Quack, quack."

When birds get up in the morning,
They always say, "Tweet, tweet."
When birds get up in the morning,
They always say, "Tweet, tweet."
Tweet, tweet, tweet,
Tweet, tweet, tweet.
When birds get up in the morning,
They always say, "Tweet, tweet."

When (*Say the baby's name and something that she says in the morning.*)

One Button

One button, two buttons,
Three buttons, four.
Five buttons, six buttons,
Seven buttons,
More.

One kiss, two kisses,
Three kisses, four.
Five kisses, six kisses,
Seven kisses,
More.
*(Say the rhyme as
you button the baby's
clothes.)*

22

DRESSING AND BATHTIME

I Brush My Teeth

I brush my teeth in the morning,
I brush my teeth in the morning,
I brush my teeth in the morning,
Every single day.

I wash my hands in the morning,
I wash my hands in the morning,
I wash my hands in the morning,
Every single day.
(Make up verses as you dress your baby and act them out.)

Tiny Tim

I had a little brother,
His name was Tiny Tim,
I put him in the bathtub
To see if he could swim.

He drank up all the water,
He ate up all the soap,
And now he's home sick in bed
With bubbles in his throat.

In came the doctor,
In came the nurse,
In came the lady
With the alligator purse,

"Measles," said the doctor,
"Mumps," said the nurse,
"Chicken pox," said the lady
With the alligator purse.

I don't want the doctor,
I don't want the nurse,
I don't want the lady
With the alligator purse.

DRESSING AND BATHTIME

Button the Buttons

Button the buttons, snap the snaps,
Hook the hooks and zip the zippers.
Tie the ties and strap the straps,
And clasp the clasps and slip the slippers.
Buckle the buckles and,
Pin the pins and
Lace the laces and
Loop the loops and
Lock the locks and
Belt the belts and
Brace the braces.

What I like best is my own skin,
That is the dress I'm always in.

A Sailor

A sailor went to sea, sea, sea,
To see what he could see, see, see.
And all that he could see, see, see,
Was the bottom of the deep, blue sea, sea, sea.

DRESSING AND BATHTIME

Where, Oh Where

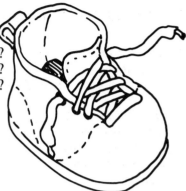

Where, oh, where are Johnny's clothes?
Where, oh, where are Johnny's clothes?
Where, oh, where are Johnny's clothes?
I see Johnny's shoe.

Put the shoe on Johnny's foot,
Put the shoe on Johnny's foot,
Put the shoe on Johnny's foot,
Shake it round and round.

(Repeat the rhyme using different articles of clothing. Substitute your baby's name as you say the rhyme.)

Slippery Soap

Slippery, slippery, slippery, soap,
Now you see it,
And now you don't.
Slide it on the arms,
One, two, three,
Now your arms are slippery.

Slide it on the legs,
One, two, three,
Now your legs are slippery.
*(Repeat the verse substituting
different body parts.)*

DRESSING AND BATHTIME

Diddle Diddle Dumpling

Diddle, diddle, dumpling,
My son John
Went to bed with his stockings on.
One shoe off,
(Shake the baby's left foot.)
And one shoe on,
(Shake the baby's right foot.)
Diddle, diddle, dumpling,
My son John.

Wake up Little Fingers

Wake up little fingers, the morning has come,
Now hold them up, every finger and thumb.
(Open your fingers and wiggle them.)
Now jump out of bed and stand up tall,
You're the tallest fingers that I ever saw.
(Hold your fingers high in the air.)
Wash your hands so clean and neat,
Come to the table so you can eat.
(Pretend to wash your hands and to eat.)
Now little fingers, run out to play,
And have a good time on this beautiful day.
(Wiggle the baby's fingers and wave good-bye.)

DRESSING AND BATHTIME

Zip, Zip, Zip

Zip, zip, zip, off it goes!
I see baby without clothes.
Zip, zip, zip,
What do I see?
Diaper on, one-two-three!

Clothes, Clothes

Clothes, clothes, where're my clothes?
Now it's time for dressing,
Clothes, clothes, where're my clothes?
Now it's time for dressing.

Socks, socks, where're my socks?
Now it's time for dressing.
Socks, socks, where're my socks?
Now it's time for dressing.
(As you say the rhyme, put on the baby's socks.)

Shoes, shoes, where're my shoes?
Now it's time for dressing.
Shoes, shoes, where're my shoes?
Now it's time for dressing.
(Put on the baby's shoes.)

(Repeat the rhyme using other articles of clothing.)

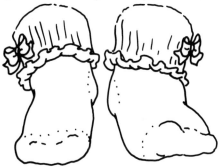

DRESSING AND BATHTIME

This Is the Way

This is the way we wash our hands,
Wash our hands,
Wash our hands.
This is the way we wash our hands,
Every single day.
(Pretend to wash your hands.)
This is the way we wash our toes,
Wash our toes,
Wash our toes.
This is the way we wash our toes,
Every single day.
(Pretend to wash your toes.
Repeat the rhyme using other body parts.)

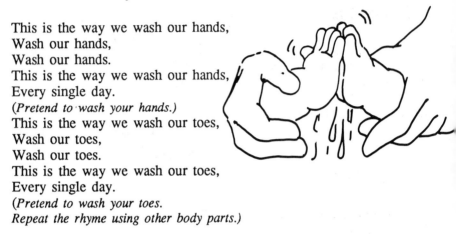

Here Comes the Rain

Here comes the rain,
Splash, splash, splash.
(Splash the tub water.)
Here comes the rain,
Drip, drip, drip.
(Drip little droplets
on the baby.)
Here comes the rain,
Pitter, patter,
(Flick your fingers in the water.)
Get the baby clean all over!
(Wash the baby with a cloth.)

DRESSING AND BATHTIME

Head and Shoulders

Here's the way this poem goes,
Head and shoulders, knees and toes,
Eyes and ears and mouth and nose,
That's the way the poem goes.
Head, shoulders, knees, toes,
Eyes, and ears, and mouth, and nose.
(Touch the appropriate part of the baby's body as you say each word. Go faster and faster.)

Five Speckled Frogs

Five little speckled frogs.
Sitting on a speckled log.
Eating the most delicious bugs,
Yuummmmmmm,Yuummmmmmm!
(Pretend to eat bugs.)
One jumped into the pool.
Where it was nice and cool.
Then there were four specked frogs.
(Pretend to jump in the pool and hold up four fingers. Keep repeating till there are no frogs left.)

DRESSING AND BATHTIME

The Shoe Game

You must pass this shoe from me to you,
You must pass this shoe and
Do just what I do.
*(Hold the baby's shoe in your hand and
put it on the baby's foot.)*

You must pass this shirt from me to you,
You must pass this shirt and
Do just what I do.
(Put the shirt on the baby.)

*(Repeat the rhyme using other
articles of clothing.)*

Motor Boat

Motor boat, motor boat,
Putt, putt, putt,
Can you make your mouth go
Putt, putt, putt?

Sailing boat, sailing boat,
Swish, swish, swish,
Can you make your mouth go
Swish, swish, swish?

Big boat, big boat,
Splash, splash, splash,
Can you make your mouth go
Splash, splash, splash?

MEALTIME

The Apple Tree

Away up high in the apple tree,
(Point upward with your index finger.)
Two red apples smiled at me.
(Smile at your baby.)
I shook that tree as hard as I could.
(Pretend to shake a tree very hard.)
Down came the apples and
M-M-M-M-M- they were good.
(Rub your tummy.)

Bubble Said The Kettle

"Bubble," said the kettle,
"Bubble," said the pot,
"Bubble, bubble, bubble,
We are very, very hot."

Shall I take you off the fire?
"No, you need not trouble.
This is just the way we talk
Bubble, bubble, bubble."
(Each time you say "bubble," push your index finger down over your lips.)

MEALTIME

This Is My Saucer

This is my saucer,
This is my cup,
And this is the way
I lift it up.
(Pick up a plastic cup.)

This is my saucer,
This is my cup,
Pour in the milk
And drink it up.
(Pretend to drink milk from a cup.)

There Was a Little House

There was a little house
And it had a little door
And I knocked on the knocker,
1-2-3-4.
Out came a little lady,
She curtsied low to me,
And said, "Will you come inside,
And have a cup of tea?"

MEALTIME

A Lemon and a Pickle

Last night and the night before,
A lemon and a pickle
Came knocking at my door.
(Hold up two fists and pretend to knock at a door.)
I went down to let them in,
They bopped me on the head with a rolling pin.
(Hit one fist on the other when you say "bopped.")

All Around the Kitchen

All around the kitchen,
Cocky doodle doo.
All around the kitchen,
Cocky doodle doo.
Put your hand on your head,
Cocky doodle doo.
Put your hand on your nose,
Cocky doodle doo.
Put your hand on your cheek,
Cocky doodle doo.
*(Keep adding body parts
to the verse.)*

MEALTIME

What's for Dinner

What's for dinner? What's for dinner?
Irish stew, Irish stew,
Sloppy semolina, sloppy semolina,
No thank you, no thank you.
(Tune: "Frere Jacques"
Make up your own words to put in the song.)

Little Sausage

I had a little sausage, a bonny, bonny, sausage,
I put it in the oven for my tea.
I went down to the cellar
To get the salt and pepper,
And the bonny little sausage
Ran after me.
(Tickle the baby from the top of her head to the bottom of her toes.)

MEALTIME

Peas Porridge Hot

Peas porridge hot,
Peas porridge cold,
Peas porridge in the pot,
Nine days old.
(Clap the baby's hands as
you say the rhyme.)
Some like it hot,
Some like it cold,
Some like it in the pot,
Nine days old.
(Take your index finger and thumb
and squeeze the baby's nose gently)

Canty Canty Custard

Canty, canty Custard,
Ate a pound of mustard.
Hurt his tongue and
Home did run,
Canty, canty Custard.

Splishy, splashy Custard,
Spilled a jar of mustard.
Picked it up
With broom and mop,
Splishy, splashy Custard.

MEALTIME

Peanut Butter

Peanut butter, peanut butter,
Jelly, jelly.
Peanut butter, peanut butter,
Jelly, jelly.

First you take the peanuts and you
Crush them, crush them.
First you take the peanuts and you
Crush them, crush them.
(Pretend to crush peanuts in your hand.)

Then you take the grapes and you
Smash them, smash them.
Then you take the grapes and you
Smash them, smash them.
(Pretend to smash grapes in your hand.)

Then you take the bread and you
Spread it, spread it.
Then you take the bread and you
Spread it, spread it.
(Pretend to spread peanut butter on bread.)

Then you take the sandwich and you
Eat it, eat it.
Then you take the sandwich and you
Eat it, eat it.
(Pretend to eat a sandwich.)

Peanut butter, peanut butter,
Jelly, jelly.
Peanut butter, peanut butter,
Jelly, jelly.
(Say the words like you have a mouth full of peanut butter.)

MEALTIME

Little Miss Muffet

(A different version)

Little Miss Muffet,
Sat on her tuffet,
Eating her curds and whey.
Along came a spider,
Who sat down beside her,
And said, "What a very nice day."

Little Jack Horner

Little Jack Horner,
Sat in a corner
Eating a Christmas pie.
(Pretend to be eating a pie.)
He stuck in his thumb,
(Pretend to stick in your thumb.)
And pulled out a plum,
(Hold your thumb high in the air.)
And said, "What a good boy am I!")
(Point your thumb to your chest.)

MEALTIME

Little Fishes

Little fishes in a brook,
(Move your hands like fishes swimming.)
Mommy caught them on a hook.
(Clap your hands together.)
Daddy fried them in a pan.
(Make a hissing sound like fish frying.)
Johnnie eats them as fast as he can.
(Substitute the baby's name and pretend to eat.)

Little King Pippin

Little King Pippin,
He built a fine hall.
Pie crust and pastry crust,
That was the wall.
The windows were made of
Black pudding and white,
And slated with pancakes,
You ne'er saw the like!

MEALTIME

Little Tommy Tucker

Little Tommy Tucker,
Sings for his supper,
What shall we give him?
White bread and butter.
How shall he cut it
Without e'er a knife?
How will he be married
Without e're a wife?
(Substitute the baby's name for Tommy Tucker.)

Betty Botter

Betty Botter bought some butter.
"But" she said, "this butter's bitter.
If I put it in my batter,
It will make by batter bitter.
But a bit of better butter,
Will make my batter better."

So she bought a bit of butter,
Better than her bitter butter
And she put it in her batter,
And it made her batter better.
So 'twas better Betty Botter,
Bought a bit of better butter.

MEALTIME

Baby and I

Baby and I,
Were baked in a pie.
The gravy was wonderfully hot.
We had nothing to pay
To the baker that day,
And so we crept out of the pot.
Creep, creep, creep, creep.
(Cup one hand on a table and creep the fingers of your other hand in and out.)

The Muffin Man

Oh, do you know the Muffin Man,
The Muffin Man, the Muffin Man,
Oh, do you know the Muffin Man,
That lives in Drury Lane?
(Shake your index finger back and forth.)

Oh, yes I know the Muffin Man,
The Muffin Man, the Muffin Man,
Oh, yes I know the Muffin Man,
That lives in Drury Lane.
(Shake your head yes.)

MEALTIME

Five Currant Buns

Five currant buns in the baker's shop,
Big and round with some sugar on the top.
Along came Tom with a penny to pay
Who bought a currant bun
And took it right away.
Four currant buns in the baker's shop....
Three currant buns in the baker's shop...
Two...
One...

No currant buns in the baker's shop,
Big and round with some sugar on the top.
No one came with a penny to pay,
So close the baker's shop and have a baking day.

Hot Cross Buns

Hot cross buns,
Hot cross buns,
One-a-penny, two-a-penny,
Hot cross buns.
If you have no daughters,
Give them to your sons.
One-a-penny, two-a-penny,
Hot cross buns.
And if you haven't any
Of these pretty little elves,
You cannot do better,
Than eat them yourselves.

MEALTIME

Handy Spandy

Handy, Spandy, Jack-a-dandy,
Loves plum cake and sugar candy.
He bought some at the grocer's shop,
And out he came, hop, hop, hop!

Handy, Spandy, Jack-a-dandy,
Loves carrot cake and chocolate candy.
He bought some at the grocery store,
And he was happy ever more.

Make a Pancake

Make a pancake, pat, pat, pat;
(Pat the baby's hands together.)
Do not make it fat, fat, fat;
(Stretch the baby's hands.)
You must make it flat, flat, flat.
(Pat the baby's hands together.)
Make a pancake just like that!
(Clap the baby's hands together.)

MEALTIME

Two Little Hot Dogs

Two little hot dogs frying in a pan,
The grease got so hot and one went BAM!

One little hot dog frying in the pan,
One went POP! and one went BAM!

No little hot dogs frying in the pan,
The grease got hot and the pan went BAM!
(Each time you say "BAM," give the baby a kiss.)

M-m-m-m Smells So Good

M-m-m-m, smells so good,
What's that food that smells so good?
Is it a potato?
Or is it a tomato?
M-m-m-m, smells so good.

M-m-m-m, smells so good
What's that food that smells so good?
Is it broccoli?
Or is it macaroni?
M-m-m-m, smells so good.
(Substitute your own foods to go in the rhyme.)

CUDDLING

Love Somebody

Love somebody, yes I do,
Love somebody, yes I do,
Love somebody, yes I do,
Love somebody, can you guess who?
(Rock baby back and forth as you say the chant.)

Love somebody, yes I do,
Love somebody, yes I do,
Love somebody, yes I do,
Love somebody, and it's YOU!
(Give the baby a big kiss.)

Counting

One for sorrow,
Two for joy,
Three for a kiss,
And four for a boy.
Five for silver,
Six for gold,
Seven for a secret,
Never to be told.
Eight for a letter
From over the sea,
Nine for my baby
As sweet as can be.

CUDDLING

Baby Walks

This is the way my baby walks,
And this is the way she walks you see.
(Walk your baby.)

This is the way my baby hops,
And this is the way she hops you see.
(Hop your baby.)

This is the way my baby runs,
And this is the way she runs you see.
(Run your baby.)

This is the way my baby talks,
And this is the way she talks you see.
Mamamamamama.
Dadadadadada.

Little Jack-a-Dandy

Little Jack-a-Dandy,
Has a stick of candy,
Every time he takes a bite,
A piece goes quickly out of sight.

Happy, happy, Jack-a-Dandy,
Yum, yum, yum, yum, yum.

CUDDLING

Sally, Go Round the Moon

Sally, go round the stars,
Sally, go round the moon,
*(Hold the baby close to you and walk
in a circle.)*
Sally, go round the chimney pots,
On a Sunday afternoon.
(Walk the opposite way.)
Whoops, Sally,
Whoops, Sally,
Whoops, Sally.
*(Hold the baby high in the air
and substitute the baby's name
for "Sally.")*

I'm Very Very Tall

I'm very, very tall,
I'm very, very small,
Sometimes tall,
Sometimes small,
Guess what I am now?
*(Hold the baby high or low
according to the word
in the rhyme.)*

CUDDLING

This Little Cow

This little cow eats grass,
This little cow eats hay,
This little cow looks over the hedge,
This little cow runs away.
And this little cow does nothing at all,
But lie in the fields all day!
(*Use different fingers or toes as you say this rhyme.*)
Let's chase this little cow,
Chase, chase, chase, chase, chase.
(*Tickle the baby all over.*)

Windshield Wiper

Windshield wiper, windshield wiper,
What do you do all day?
Swish, swish, swish, swish,
I wipe the rain away.

Honking horn, honking horn,
What do you do all day?
I tell the people honk, honk,
Please get out of my way.

Vacuum cleaner, vacuum cleaner,
What do you do all day?
Buzz, buzz, buzz, buzz,
I suck the dirt away.

Little lips, little lips,
What do you do all day?
I kiss my little baby,
Hip, hip, hooray.

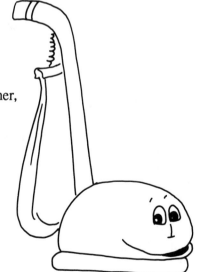

CUDDLING

Tommy Thumbs

Tommy thumbs up,
(Put thumbs up.)
Tommy thumbs down,
(Put thumbs down.)
Tommy thumbs dancing,
All around the town.
(Dance thumbs in the air.)
Dance them on your shoulders,
(Put thumbs on your shoulders.)
Dance them on your head,
(Put thumbs on your head.)
Dance them on your knees,
(Put thumbs on your knees.)
And tuck them into bed.
(Hide your hands behind your back.)

Peter pointer up,
(Repeat the rhyme using your pointer finger.)

Finger family up,
(Repeat again using all of your fingers.)

Jack in the Box

I'm Jack in the box,
I'm Jack in the box,
I crouch so very low.
Turn the handle,
Round and round,
And up I go.

I'm Jack in the box,
I'm Jack in the box.
Just turn the handle,
And up I pop.

CUDDLING

This Little Baby

This little baby rocked in the cradle,
(Pretend to be rocking a baby.)
This little baby jumped in bed,
(Jump.)
This little baby crawled on the carpet,
(Crawl on the floor.)
This little baby bumped her head.
(Hit your hand on your head.)
This little baby played hide'n'seek,
(Hide your face behind your hands.)
Where's that baby?
Peek - a - boo!!

Dance to Your Daddy

Dance to your daddy,
My bonnie laddie,
Dance to your daddy,
My bonnie lamb.
Dance to your daddy,
My bonnie laddie,
I'll play with you,
As much as I can.

CUDDLING

Ibble Obble

Ibble, obble. black bobble,
Ibble, obble, out.
(Move your index finger over your lips as you say the words.)
Turn a little dishcloth,
Inside out.
(Twist your wrists as if wringing out a wet cloth.)

If it's not dirty,
Turn it back again,
(Wring out the cloth again.)
Ibble, obble, black bobble,
Ibble, obble, out.

Froggie

A froggie sat on a log,
A-weeping for his daughter.
(Bounce your baby on your knee.)
His eyes were red,
His tears he shed,
(Say in a sad voice.)
And he FELL right in the water.
*(Gently slide your baby
between your knees.)*

CUDDLING

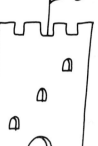

Climbing the Tower

I am climbing up the tower,
(Start climbing up the baby's arm with your fingers.)
I am going to ring the bell.
(Keep climbing up the arm.)
Ding, ding, ding, ding.
(Put your hands on the baby's shoulders and move the baby back and forth.)

Round and Round

Round and round the garden,
Went a teddy bear.
One step,
Two steps,
Jump up in the air.
(Hold the baby close to you as you turn in a circle.)

Round and round the lighthouse,
Up the spiral stair.
One step,
Two steps,
Right up in the air.
(Hold the baby close to you as you pretend to walk up the stairs.)

Round and round the haystack,
Went a little mouse.
One step,
Two steps,
In his little house.
(Hold the baby close to you and on the last line, swing the baby under your legs.)

CUDDLING

Wiggle Wiggle

Wiggle, wiggle, wiggle,
Little finger,
(Wiggle your index finger.)
Wiggle, wiggle, wiggle,
In the air.
(Hold your index finger in the air.)
Wiggle, wiggle, wiggle,
Little finger,
Wiggle all around,
And put it there.
(On the word "there," touch the baby's nose.)

Baby's Face

Here are baby's eyes to look around,
(Touch the baby's eyes.)
Here are baby's ears to listen to a sound,
(Touch the baby's ears.)
Here is baby's nose to smell something sweet,
(Touch the baby's nose.)
Here is baby's mouth that likes to eat.
*(Touch the baby's mouth and
give the baby a hug.)*

CUDDLING

The Little Flea

The little flea went walking,
(Walk your fingers on your baby.)
To see what he could see,
*(Move your fingers all over the baby,
stopping and starting.)*
And all the little flea could see,
WAS......
A little little tummy.
(Tickle baby on the tummy.)

Bears Eat Honey

Bears eat honey,
Cows eat corn,
What do you eat,
When you get up in the morn?

Monkeys eat bananas,
Cows eat corn,
What do you eat,
When you get up in the morn?

Baby eats oatmeal,
Cows eat corn,
What do you eat,
When you get up in the morn?
(Substitute child's name for "baby.")

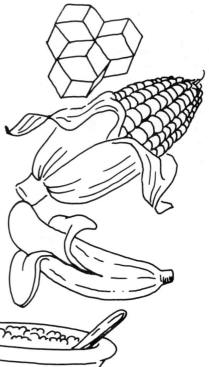

CUDDLING

Hop Hop Hop

Hop, hop, hop,
To the butcher's shop,
(Hold the baby close to you as you hop.)
I dare not stay any longer,
(Hop back to where you started from.)
For if I do, my mommy will say,
"I'm gonna kiss you every day."
(Give the baby lots of kisses.)

Dance a Merry Jig

This little pig danced a merry, merry jig,
This little pig ate candy,
This little pig wore a blue and yellow wig,
This little pig was a dandy,
But this little pig never grew very big,
And they called her itty bitty Mandy.
(Touch a toe or finger as you say the rhyme. Substitute the child's name for "Mandy.")

CUDDLING

This Is the Way the Ladies Ride

This is the way the ladies ride,
Bounce, bounce, bounce.
(Bounce the baby on your knee.)

This is the way the gentlemen ride,
Boom, boom, boom.
(Bounce the baby a little faster.)

This is the way the farmers ride,
Trot, trot, trot.
(Keep the baby on your knees and lift her legs up one at a time.)

This is the way the babies ride,
Wheeeeeee!
(Hold the baby high in the air.)

The Kissing Rhyme

Up, up, up, in the sky like this,
(Hold the baby high in the air.)
Down, down, down, for a great big kiss.
(Bring the baby down for a kiss.)
Up like this,
Down for a kiss,
You're a special baby.
*(Hold the baby close to you
and cuddle her.)*

CUDDLING

Knock at the Door

Knock at the door,
(Tap the baby on the forehead.)
Pull the bell,
(Gently pull a lock of hair.)
Lift the latch,
*(Touch the tip of
the baby's nose.)*
And walk in,
(Touch the baby's lips.)
Go down into the basement.
(Tickle the baby's throat.)

Mama Told Me

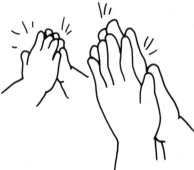

My mama told ME,
To tell YOU,
To clap your hands,
Just like I do.
*(Clap your hands and
then clap the baby's hands.)*

My mama told ME,
To tell YOU,
To shake your head,
Just like I do.
(Shake your head back and forth and then do the same with the baby.)

Tap your toes...
Bend your knees...
Throw a kiss...

OUTDOOR PLAY

Grasshopper Green

Grasshopper Green is a comical chap,
He lives on the best of fare.
Bright little trousers, jacket, and cap,
These are his summer wear.
Out in the meadow he loves to go,
Playing away in the sun.
It's hoppity, skippity, high and low,
Summer's the time for fun.

Grasshopper Green has a quaint little house,
It's under the hedge so gay.
Grandmother Spider, as still as a mouse,
Watches him over the way.
Gladly he's calling the children, I know,
Out in the beautiful sun,
It's hoppity, skippity, high and low,
Summer's the time for fun.

The Wind

I can blow like the wind,
(Blow gently.)
I can bring the rain,
(Move fingers like raindrops.)
When I blow very softly,
I can whisper my name.
(Whisper the baby's name.)

OUTDOOR PLAY

Dr. Foster

Dr. Foster went to Gloucester,
In a shower of rain,
He stepped in a puddle,
Up to his middle,
And never went there again.

If All of the Raindrops

If all of the raindrops,
Were lemon drops and gum drops,
Oh, what a rain it would be.
I'd stand outside,
With my mouth open wide,
Uh-uh-uh-uh-uh-uh-uh,
Uh-uh-uh.
If all of the raindrops,
Were lemon drops and gum drops,
Oh, what a rain it would be.

If all of the snowflakes,
Were chocolate bars and milk shakes,
Oh, what a snow it would be,
I'd stand outside,
With my mouth open wide,
Uh-uh-uh-uh-uh-uh-uh,
Uh-uh-uh.
If all of the snowflakes,
Were chocolate bars and milk shakes,
Oh, what a snow, it would be.

OUTDOOR PLAY

Rain Rain

Rain, rain,
(Repeat in a softer voice.)
Falling to the ground,
(Repeat in a softer voice.)
Pitter, patter,
(Repeat in a softer voice.)
What a lovely sound.
(Repeat in a softer voice.)

Rain, rain,
(Repeat in a softer voice.)
Falling on my toys,
(Repeat in a softer voice.)
Drip, drip, drip, drip,
(Repeat in a softer voice.)
Funny sounding noise.
(Repeat in a softer voice.)

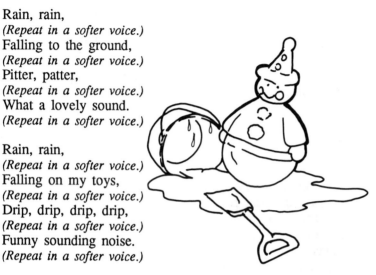

Round the Maypole

Round and round the maypole,
Merrily we go,
Singing hip-a-cherry,
Dancing as we go.
All the happy children,
Upon the village green,
Sitting in the sunshine,
Hurrah for the queen!

OUTDOOR PLAY

I'm A Walkin

I'm a walkin',walkin',walkin',
I'm a walkin',walkin',walkin',
I'm a walkin',walkin',walkin',
Then I stop!
(Walk outside and when you say the word "stop," name the object that is in front of you. For example:"tree", "house", "flower", etc.)

A Caterpillar

A caterpillar crawled to the top of a tree,
"I think I'll take a nap," said he.
Under a leaf he began to creep,
To spin his cocoon,
And he fell asleep.
All winter long he slept in his bed,
'Til Spring came along one day and said,
"Wake up, it's time to get out of bed."
So he opened his eyes that sunshiny day,
And he was a butterfly, and he flew away.
(Make up actions to the words.)

OUTDOOR PLAY

Rain Rhymes

Rain, rain, go away,
Come again another day,
Little *(baby's name)*
Wants to play.

It's raining, it's pouring,
The old man is snoring.
He went to bed and bumped his head,
And he couldn't get up until morning.

Spring Is Coming

Spring is coming, spring is coming,
How do you think I know?
I see a flower blooming,
I know it must be so.

Spring is coming, spring is coming,
How do you think I know?
I see a blossom on the tree,
I know it must be so.

(Add your own verses with other signs of spring.)

OUTDOOR PLAY

Pussy Willow

I have a little pussy,
And her coat is silver gray,
She lives in a great wide meadow,
And she never runs away.

She always is a pussy,
She'll never be a cat,
Because - she's a pussy willow!
Now what do you think of that!

A Devonshire Rhyme

Walk fast in snow,
In frost walk slow,
And still as you go,
Tread on your toe.
When frost and snow are both together,
Sit by the fire and spare shoe leather.

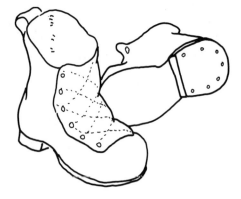

OUTDOOR PLAY

Misty Moisty Morn

Misty, moisty was the morn,
Chilly was the weather,
There I met an old, old man,
Dressed all in leather.

Dressed all in leather,
Against the wind and rain,
With "How do you do?"
And "How do you do?"
And "How do you do?" again.

Bells

"Two sticks and an apple,"
Say the bells at Whitechapel.
"Old Father Baldgate,"
Say the slow bells at Aldgate.
"Maids in white aprons,"
Say the bells at St. Catherine's.
"Oranges and lemons,"
Say the bells of St. Clement's.
(Swing the baby back and forth.)

OUTDOOR PLAY

Arabella Miller

Little Arabella Miller,
Found a furry caterpillar,
(Pretend to have a caterpillar in your hand.)
First it crawled upon her mother,
Then upon her little brother,
(Crawl your fingers up and down your arm.)
Both cried, "NAUGHTY ARABELLA,
PUT AWAY THAT CATERPILLAR!"

Seasons

In the summer leaves are rustling,
Green, green leaves are rustling,
In the summer leaves are rustling,
Rustling on the trees.

In the autumn leaves are falling,
Brown, brown leaves are falling,
In the autumn leaves are falling,
Falling from the trees.

In the winter leaves are sleeping,
Brown, brown leaves are sleeping,
In the winter leaves are sleeping,
Sleeping in the trees.

OUTDOOR PLAY

The Snowman

I made a little snowman,
I made him big and round,
I made him from a snowball,
I rolled upon the ground.

He has two eyes, a nose, a mouth,
A lovely scarf of red,
He even has some buttons,
And a hat upon his head.

Melt, melt, melt, melt,
Melt, melt, melt, melt.
(Pretend you are melting to the ground.)

Six Little Snowmen

Six little snowmen all made of snow,
(Hold up six fingers)
Six little snowmen,
Standing in a row.
(Lift your arms over your head in a circle.)
Out came the sun and stayed all day.
One little snowman melted away.
(Make a wavy motion with your hand and pretend to melt to the floor.)

Five little snowmen all made of snow,
Five little snowmen standing in a row.
Out came the sun and stayed all day.
One little snowman melted away.
(Continue with" Four little snowmen," etc.)

OUTDOOR PLAY

The Grand Old Duke of York

The grand old Duke of York
He had ten thousand men.
He marched them up the hill,
And then he marched them down again.

Now when they're up, they're up,
And when they're down, they're down.
And when they're only halfway up,
They're neither up nor down.
(Move your body up or down according to the words.)

My Feet

I can walk on my feet,
Walk, walk, walk.
I can hop on my feet,
Hop, hop, hop.
I can jump with my feet,
Jump, jump, jump.
Now sit down and rest.

I can march on my feet,
March, march, march.
I can tiptoe on my feet,
Tip, tiptoe.
I can run with my feet,
Run, run, run.
Now sit down and rest.

OUTDOOR PLAY

Cousin Peter

Last evening cousin Peter came,
Last evening cousin Peter came,
Last evening cousin Peter came,
And showed us he was here.

He knocked three times upon the door,
He knocked three times upon the door,
He knocked three times upon the door,
To show us he was here.

He wiped his feet upon the mat...
He hung his hat upon the hook...
He danced about in stocking feet...

He made a bow and said goodbye,
He made a bow and said goodbye,
He made a bow and said goodbye,
GOODBYE!
(Do the appropriate actions.)

Johnny Hammer

Johnny taps with one hammer,
One hammer, one hammer,
Johnny taps with one hammer,
Then he taps with two.

Johnny taps with two hammers...
Then he taps with three.
(Accompany the verse with fist, feet, and hand actions.)

Johnny taps with five hammers,
Then he goes to sleep.

OUTDOOR PLAY

Twinkle Twinkle

Twinkle, twinkle, little star,
How I wonder what you are.
Up above the earth so high,
Like a diamond in the sky.
Twinkle, twinkle, little star,
How I wonder what you are.
(*Put your hands high in the air and wiggle your fingers.*)

When the blazing sun is gone,
When he nothing shines upon,
Then you show your little light,
Twinkle, twinkle, all the night.

Then the traveler in the dark,
Thanks you for your tiny spark,
He could not see which way to go,
If you did not twinkle so.

In the dark blue sky you keep,
And often through my curtains peep,
For you never shut your eye,
'Til the sun is in the sky.
(*Say the chorus between each verse.*)

Lavender's Blue

Lavender's blue, dilly, dilly,
Lavender's green.
When I am king, dilly, dilly,
You shall be queen.
Call up your men, dilly, dilly,
Set them to work.
Some to the plough, dilly, dilly,
Some to the cart.
Some to make hay, dilly, dilly,
Some to cut corn.
While you and I, dilly, dilly,
Keep ourselves warm.

OUTDOOR PLAY

Caught a Rabbit

Rabbit run on the frozen ground,
Who told you so?
Rabbit run on the frozen ground,
How do you know?

I caught a rabbit, uh-huh,
I caught a rabbit, uh-huh,
I caught a rabbit, uh-huh,
I caught a rabbit, oh!

Four Little Frogs

Four little frogs,
Sitting on a well,
Two leaned over
And down they fell.
(Fall to the ground.)

Frogs jump high,
Frogs jump low,
Two little frogs,
Jump to and fro.
(Jump up and down like a frog.)

Two little frogs,
Sitting on a well,
Two leaned over
And down they fell.
(Fall to the ground.)

Frogs jump high,
Frogs jump low,
No little frogs
Jump to and fro.
(Stay on the ground and tickle your child.)

ANIMALS

I Had a Little Turtle

I had a little turtle that lived in a box,
He swam in the water,
And he climbed on the rocks.
He snapped at a mosquito,
He snapped at a flea,
He snapped at a minnow,
And he snapped at me.

He caught the mosquito,
He caught the flea,
He caught the minnow,
But he DIDN'T CATCH ME!

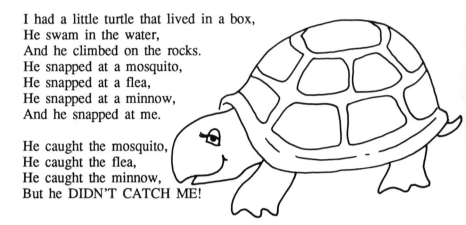

Snake Baked a Hoecake

Snake baked a hoecake,
And set a frog to watch it,
And the frog got a-nodding,
And a lizard came and stole it.
Fetch back my hoecake,
You long tailed nanny, you.
Fetch back my hoecake,
You long tailed nanny, you.

ANIMALS

Little Birdie

What does the little birdie say,
In her nest at the peak of day?
"Let me fly," says the birdie,
"Mother, please let me fly."
"Birdie dear, rest a little longer,
'Til your little wings are stronger."
So she rests and rests all day,
Then she wakes and flies away.

Baby Birdie

Here's a baby birdie,
He's hatching from his shell,
Out comes his little head,
And then comes his tail.
Now his legs are stretching,
His wings go flap, flap, flap,
Then he flies and flies and flies,
Now what do you think of that?

ANIMALS

Five Little Monkeys

Five little monkeys,
Jumping on the bed,
(Hold up five fingers.)
One jumped off and
Hurt his little head.
(Put your hand to your head.)
Papa called the doctor,
(Pretend to dial a phone.)
And the doctor said,
"No more monkeys,
Jumping on the bed!"
(Shake your finger as you say the words.)

Hey Diddle Diddle

Hey diddle diddle,
The cat and the fiddle,
The cow jumped over the moon.
The little dog laughed,
To see such sport,
And the dish ran away
With the spoon.

ANIMALS

Hop-A-Doodle

Down in the meadow,
Hop-a-doodle, hop-a-doodle,
Down in the meadow,
Hop-a-doodle doo.
Down in the meadow,
The colt began to prance,
(Gallop around while holding the baby.)
The cow began to whistle,
(Whistle.)
And the pig began to dance.
(Dance around while holding the baby.)

Pretty Butterflies

Oh, the pretty butterflies,
How they fly, how they fly.
Oh, the pretty butterflies,
How they circle in the sky.

Oh, they-wind in and out,
In and out, in and out.
Oh, the pretty butterflies,
See them flying all about.
(Fly around like a butterfly.)

ANIMALS

Teddy Bear

Teddy bear, teddy bear,
Turn around.
Teddy bear, teddy bear,
Touch the ground.

Teddy bear, teddy bear,
Reach up high,
Teddy bear, teddy bear,
Wink one eye.

Teddy bear, teddy bear,
Slap your knees.
Teddy bear, teddy bear,
Sit down please.
(Do the actions as you say the words.)

The Snail

Hand in hand you see us well,
Creep like a snail into his shell.
(Cup one hand and creep fingers of the other hand into it.)
Ever nearer, ever nearer,
Ever closer, ever closer,
Very snug indeed you dwell,
Snail within your tiny shell.

ANIMALS

The Animals Are My Friends

The animals are my friends,
The animals are my friends.
We all live together,
In cold and sunny weather,
The animals are my friends.

Be courteous and helpful too,
You could be friends with a kangaroo.
An elephant or tall giraffe,
Can be your friend and make you laugh.

The animals are my friends,
The animals are my friends.
We all live together,
In cold and sunny weather,
The animals are my friends.

Duck in the Pond

A duck in the pond,
A fish in the pool,
Whoever reads this,
Is a big April Fool.

ANIMALS

I Had a Little Doggy

I had a little doggy that used to sit and beg,
But doggy tumbled down the stairs and broke his little leg.
Oh, doggy, I will nurse you and try to make you well,
And you shall have a collar with a little silver bell.

Oh, doggy, don't you think that you should very faithful be,
For having such a loving friend to comfort you as me?
And when your leg is better, and you can run and play,
We'll have a scamper in the fields and see them making hay.

Robins

What do robins whisper about
From their homes in the elms and birches?
I've tried to figure the riddle out,
But still in my mind is many a doubt,
In spite of deep researches.

While all the world is in silence deep
In the twilight of early dawning,
They begin to chirp and twitter and peep
As if they were talking in their sleep,
At three o'clock in the morning.

ANIMALS

Furry Squirrel

I'm a fur, fur, furry squirrel,
With a bush, bush, bushy tail,
And I scamper here and there,
Scamper everywhere,
Looking for some nuts.

I've got nuts on my nose,
Nuts in my toes,
Nuts on my head,
Nuts in my bed,
Nuts in my paws,
Nuts in my jaws,
Crack, crack, POP!

Visiting the Farm

I went to visit the farm one day,
I saw a cow across the way.
And what do you think I heard it say?
Moo, moo, moo.

I went to visit the farm one day,
I saw a duck across the way,
And what do you think I heard it say?
Quack, quack, quack.
(Repeat adding new animals.)

77

ANIMALS

Did You Feed My Cow?

Did you feed my cow?
Yes maam!
Did you feed her now?
Yes maam!
What did you feed her?
Corn and hay.
What did you feed her?
Corn and hay.
Did you milk my cow?
Yes maam!
Did you milk her now?
Yes maam!
How did you milk her?
Squish, squish, squish,
How did you milk her?
Squish, squish, squish.

Little Gray Squirrel

Little gray squirrel,
Swish your bushy tail.
Little gray squirrel,
Swish your bushy tail.
Wrinkle up your little nose,
Hold a nut between your toes.
Little gray squirrel,
Swish your bushy tail.

ANIMALS

Flies in the Buttermilk

Flies in the buttermilk,
Shoo fly, shoo,
Flies in the buttermilk,
Shoo fly, shoo,
Flies in the buttermilk,
Shoo fly, shoo,
Skip to my Lou, my darling.
(Repeat using the following:
Ants in the orange juice....
Crickets in the lemonade....
Babies in the chocolate milk.)

Bought Me a Cat

Bought me a cat and the cat pleased me,
Fed my cat under yonder tree.
Cat said "Meow, meow."

Bought me a pig and the pig pleased me,
Fed my pig under yonder tree.
Pig said "Oink, oink,"
Cat said "Meow, meow."

Bought me a horse and the horse pleased me,
Fed my horse under yonder tree.
Horse said "chipsy chopsy."
(Repeat the last lines of the previous verses.)

ANIMALS

Animal Fair

I went to the animal fair,
The birds and the beasts were there.
The old baboon,
By the light of the moon,
Was combing his auburn hair.

The monkey went kerplunk,
And stepped on the elephant's trunk.
The elephant sneezed,
And fell on his knees,
And that was the end of the monk,
The monk, the monk, the monk.

The Elephant

The elephant goes like this and that,
He's terribly big,
And he's terribly fat.
He has no fingers,
And he has no toes,
But goodness gracious,
What a big nose!!

ANIMALS

Animal Song

Alligator, hedge hog,
Anteater, bear,
Rattlesnake, buffalo,
Anaconda, hare.

Bull frog, woodchuck,
Wolverine, goose,
Whippoorwill, chipmunk,
Jackal, moose.

Mud Turtle, whale,
Glow worm, bat,
Salamander, snail,
Maltese cat.

Rat-A-Tat-Tat

Rat-a-tat-tat.
Who is that?
Only Grandma's pussycat.
What do you want?
A pint of milk.
Where is your money?
In my pocket.
Where is your pocket?
I forgot it.
Oh, you silly pussycat!
*(Tickle the baby as you
say the last line.)*

ANIMALS

The Animals Went in Two by Two

The animals went in two by two,
Hurrah, hurrah!
The animals went in two by two,
Hurrah, hurrah!
The animals went in two by two,
The elephant and the kangaroo,
And they all went into the ark
To get out of the rain.

The animals went in three by three,
The wasp, the ant, and the bumble bee.

The animals went in four by four,
The great hippopotamus stuck in the door.

Five Little Robins

Five little robins up in a tree,
Father, mother and babies three.
(Start with the baby's thumb and touch all five fingers.)

Father caught a bug,
Mother caught a worm,
This one got the bug,
This one got the worm,
This one said, "Now it's my turn."
(Start with the baby's thumb and end with her little finger.)

SINGING

If You're Happy

If you're happy and you know it,
Clap your hands.
(Clap your hands two times.)
If you're happy and you know it,
Clap your hands.
(Clap your hands two times.)
If you're happy and you know it,
Then your smile will surely show it,
If you're happy and you know it,
Clap your hands.
(Clap your hands two times.)

If you're happy and you know it,
Stomp your feet...
Wiggle your ears...
Stick out your tongue
(Make up your own ideas.)

You Are My Sunshine

You are my sunshine,
My only sunshine,
You make me happy,
When skies are gray.
You'll never know dear,
How much I love you,
Please don't take,
My sunshine away.

SINGING

Popeye

I'm Popeye the sailor man,
(Clap your hands two times.)
I live in a caravan.
(Clap your hands two times.)
I opened the door,
And fell flat on the floor,
(Fall down on the floor.)
I'm Popeye the sailor man.
(Clap your hands two times.)

I'm Popeye the garbage man,
I live in the garbage can.
I like to go swimmin,
With pickles and lemons,
I'm Popeye the garbage man.

I'm a Little Teapot

I'm a little teapot,
Short and stout,
Here is my handle,
Here is my spout.
When I get all steamed up,
Then I shout,
"Tip me over and pour me out."

I'm a tube of toothpaste,
On the shelf,
I get so lonely, all by myself.
When it comes to night time,
Then I shout,
"Lift my lid and squeeze me out."

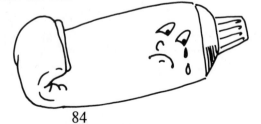

SINGING

On Top of Spaghetti

On top of spaghetti,
All covered with cheese,
I lost my poor meatball
When somebody sneezed.

It rolled off the table,
And on to the floor,
and then my poor meatball
Rolled out of the door.

It rolled in the garden,
And under a bush,
And then my poor meatball
Was nothing but mush.

The mush was so tasty,
As tasty can be,
And early next summer
It grew into a tree.

The tree was all covered,
With beautiful moss,
And on it grew meatballs
With tomato sauce.

If you like spaghetti,
All covered with cheese,
Hold on to your meat ball,
If you have to sneeze.

Buffalo Gals

Buffalo gals, won't you come out tonight,
Come out tonight, come out tonight?
Buffalo gals, won't you come out tonight,
And dance by the light of the moon?
(Dance with your baby.)

SINGING

The Wheels on the Bus

The wheels on the bus go round and round,
Round and round, round and round.
The wheels on the bus go round and round,
All through the town.

The kids on the bus go up and down.
The door on the bus goes open and shut.
The wipers on the bus go swish, swish, swish.
The baby on the bus goes waa, waa, waa.

Boom Boom

Boom, boom, ain't it great to be crazy?
Boom, boom, ain't it great to be nuts?
Silly and foolish all day long,
Boom, boom, ain't it great to be crazy?

A horse and a flea and three blind mice,
Were sitting on the curbstone shooting dice.
The horsie slipped and fell on the flea.
"Whoops!" said the flea,
"There's a horsie on me."

SINGING

Pop Goes the Weasel

All around the cobbler's bench,
The monkey chased the weasel.
The monkey thought 'twas all in fun,
Pop! goes the weasel.
(Clap on "pop.")

A penny for a spool of thread,
A penny for a needle.
That's the way the money goes,
Pop! goes the weasel.
(Clap on "pop.")

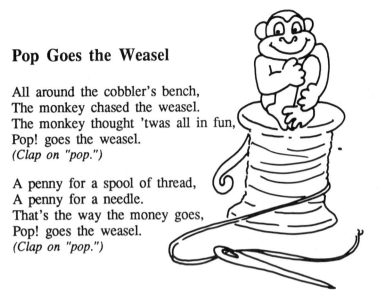

Yankee Doodle

Yankee Doodle went to town,
Riding on a pony.
He stuck a feather in his cap,
And called it macaroni.
Yankee Doodle doodle doo,
Yankee Doodle dandy,
All the lassies are so smart,
And sweet as sugar candy.

SINGING

One Finger

One finger, one thumb, keep moving,
One finger, one thumb, keep moving,
One finger, one thumb, keep moving,
We'll all be merry and bright.

One finger, one thumb, one arm,
One leg, keep moving....

One finger, one thumb, one arm,
One leg, stand up, sit down,
Nod your head, turn around,
Keep moving....

Did You Ever See a Lassie

Did you ever see a lassie,
A lassie, a lassie,
Did you ever see a lassie,
Go this way and that?
Go this way and that way,
And this way and that way,
Did you ever see a lassie,
Go this way and that?

Did you ever see a mommy?
(Repeat the verse.)

Did you ever see a daddy?
(Repeat the verse.)

SINGING

Down by the Station

Down by the station,
Early in the morning,
See the little puffer bellies,
All in a row.
See the station master
Turn the little handle,
Puff puff, choo choo,
Off they go.
(Change your voice for puff and choo.)

Heigh Ho

Heigh ho, heigh ho,
It's off to work we go.
We'll play with toys,
And make some noise,
Heigh ho, heigh ho, heigh ho.
Heigh ho, heigh ho,
It's off to work we go.
We'll have a day of fun and play,
Heigh ho, heigh ho.

Heigh ho, heigh ho,
It's off to bed we go.
We'll brush our teeth,
And wash our face,
Heigh ho, heigh ho, heigh ho.
Heigh ho, heigh ho,
It's off to bed we go.
We'll kiss good night,
And close our eyes,
Heigh ho, heigh ho.

SINGING

Dinah

Someone's in the kitchen with Dinah,
Someone's in the kitchen,
I know, I know.
Someone's in the kitchen with Dinah,
Strumming on the old banjo.
(Substitute the baby's name for Dinah.)

Fee, fi, fiddle-ee-i-o,
Fee, fi, fiddle-ee-i-o-o-o-o.
Fee, fi, fiddle-ee-i-o,
Strumming on the old banjo.

The Ants

The ants go marching one by one,
Hurrah, hurrah.
The ants go marching one by one,
Hurrah, hurrah.
The ants go marching one by one,
The little one stopped to suck his thumb,
And they all went marching down
To the earth to get out of the rain,
Boom, Boom.

Two by two - tie his shoe,
Three by three - climb a tree,
Four by four - knock at the door,
Five by five - learn to drive.

SINGING

This Old Man

This old man, he played one,
He played knick, knack on my thumb.
With a knick, knack, paddy whack,
Give your dog a bone,
This old man came rolling home.
(Roll your fists over each other.)

This old man, he played two,
He played knick, knack on my shoe.
With a knick, knack, paddy whack,
Give your dog a bone,
This old man came rolling home.

Three-knee,
Four-door,
Five-hive.

Baa Baa Black Sheep

Baa, baa black sheep,
Have you any wool?
Yes, sir, yes sir,
Three bags full.

One for my master,
One for my dame,
One for the little boy
That lives in down the lane.
(Substitute the baby's name and your own street.)

SINGING

Clementine

Oh my darling, oh my darling,
Oh my darling baby mine,
I will always love my darling,
Love my darling baby mine.

I will kiss you, I will hug you,
Oh my darling baby mine,
I will always love my darling,
Love my darling baby mine.

I will rock you, I will pat you,
Oh my darling baby mine,
I will always love my darling,
Love my darling baby mine.

Polly Wolly Doodle

Oh, I went down south,
For to see my Sal
Singing polly, wolly, doodle,
All the day.
My Sal she is a pretty gal
Singing polly, wolly, doodle,
All the day.
(Hold the baby close and dance around.)
Fare thee well, fare thee well,
Fare thee well, my fairy fay.
Oh, I'm going to Louisiana,
For to see my Susie Anna
Singing polly, wolly, doodle,
All the day.

SINGING

Head and Shoulders

Head and shoulders, knees and toes,
Knees and toes,
Head and shoulders, knees and toes,
Knees and toes,
Eyes and mouth,
And ears and nose,
Head and shoulders, knees and toes,
Knees and toes.

She'll Be Comin Around the Mountain

She'll be comin around the mountain
When she comes.
She'll be comin around the mountain
When she comes.
She'll be comin around the mountain,
She'll be comin around the mountain,
She'll be comin around the mountain
When she comes.

She'll be drivin six white horses
When she comes.
(Repeat verse.)

And we'll all go out to meet her
When she comes.
(Repeat verse.)

And we'll all have chicken and dumplings
When she comes.
(Make up appropriate actions to accompany the verse.)

SINGING

Kookaburra

Kookaburra sits in the old gum tree.
Merry, merry king of the bush is he.
Laugh, Kookaburra,
Laugh, Kookaburra,
Gay your life must be.

Kookaburra sits in the old gum tree.
Eating all the gum drops he can see.
Stop, Kookaburra,
Stop, Kookaburra,
Leave some there for me.

Down in the Valley

Down in the valley,
The valley so low,
Hear the wind blow dear,
Hear the wind blow.

Roses love sunshine,
Violets love dew,
Angels in heaven
Know I love you.

Know I love you dear,
Know I love you,
Angels in heaven
Know I love you.

SINGING

Skinnamarinky Dinky Dink

Skinnamarinky dinky dink,
Skinnmarinky doo,
I love you.
(Point to your eye and then to your baby.)

Skinnmarinky dinky dink,
Skinnmarinky doo,
I love you.
(Point to your eye and then to your baby.)

I love you in the morning,
And in the afternoon.
I love you in the evening,
Underneath the moon.

Skinnamarinky dinky dink,
Skinnamarinky doo,
I love you.
(Point to your eye and then to your baby.)

Fleas

On my toe there is a flea,
Now he's climbing on my knee,
Past my tummy, past my nose,
On my head where my hair grows.
(Sing up the scale.)

On my head there is a flea,
Now he's climbing down on me,
Past my tummy, past my knee,
On my toe,
TAKE THAT YOU FLEA!
(Sing down the scale and tickle the baby's toe.)

LAUGHING AND HAVING FUN

Dog Named Rover

As I was walking down the street,
(Lie the baby on her back.
Move her legs back and forth.)
I saw a dog named Rover.
"Come on Rover, play with me
(Move the baby's hands in a beckoning motion.)
And then we'll both turn over."
(Turn the baby over onto her tummy.)

Piggy, Piggy

Piggy, piggy, where are you?
(Wiggle the baby's big toe.)
Piggy, piggy, where's your shoe?
(Shake the baby's foot.)
Piggy, piggy, googie goo,
(Kiss the baby's toe.)
I love my little piggy.
(Pick up the baby and cuddle her.)

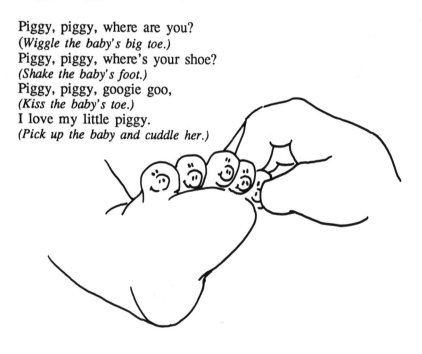

LAUGHING AND HAVING FUN

Higglety, Pigglety, Pop!

Higglety, pigglety, pop!
The dog has eaten the mop.
The pig's in a hurry,
The cat's in a flurry,
Higglety, pigglety, pop!
(Each time you say "pop," rub noses with the baby.)

Fuzzy Wuzzy

Fuzzy Wuzzy was a bear,
Fuzzy Wuzzy had no hair.
Fuzzy Wuzzy
Wasn't fuzzy,
Wuzzy!

LAUGHING AND HAVING FUN

Inky Dinky

Inky dinky, inky dinky,
Inky dinky, boo.
Inky dinky, inky dinky,
I love you.
Inkety dinkety, inkety dinkety,
Inkety dinkety, boo.
Inkety dinkety, inkety dinkety,
I love you.

Where Do You Think the Baby Lives?

Where do you think the baby lives?
Where do you think the baby lives?
Round and round and
Round and round and
Up into her house.

(Hold the baby's palm in your hand. Circle her palm with your index finger. When you come to the words "up into her house," crawl up the baby's arm and tickle her under the neck.)

LAUGHING AND HAVING FUN

Bumble Bee

Bumble bee is on your nose,
Bumble bee is on your toes.
On your nose,
On your toes,
Bzzzzzzzzzz.....BOO!
(Tickle the baby on her tummy.)

Build a House

Build a house up, build it high,
(Place your fists one on top of the other.)
Point the chimney to the sky.
(Stretch up a pointing finger.)
See the roof,
(Make your hands into a roof shape.)
See the floor,
(Make your hands into a flat shape.)
See a little yellow door.
See a father making bread,
(Work your hands in
a mixing, kneading action.)
See a baby going to bed.
(Rest your head on your folded hands.)
See the children all at play,
Dancing, dancing all the day.
(Run your fingers over your lap.)

LAUGHING AND HAVING FUN

Sounds Around the House

The clock is on the dresser,
Tick, tick, tock.
The baby's in the cradle,
Rock, rock, rock.
The rain is on the window,
Pitter, patter, pat.
The sun is coming out,
Clap, clap, clap.

To Market, to Market

To market, to market, to buy a fat pig,
Home again, home again, jiggity jig.
(Bounce the baby up and down on your knee.)

To market, to market, to buy a fat hog,
Home again, home again, jiggity jog.
(Keep bouncing the baby.)

To market, to market, to buy a new gown,
Home again, home again,
Whoops! The horse fell down.
*(Straighten your legs
and slide the baby downward.)*

LAUGHING AND HAVING FUN

Baby's Fingers

Where, oh, where are baby's fingers?
Where, oh, where are baby's toes?
Where's the baby's belly button?
Round and round it goes.

Where, oh, where are baby's ears?
Where, oh, where is baby's nose?
Where's the baby's belly button?
Round and round it goes.
(*Touch the baby's body parts as you name them.*)

Clippety Clop

Clippety clippety clippety clop,
Over the hills we go.
(*Move the baby gently up and down.*)
Jumping up,
(*Lift the baby high in the air.*)
Jumping down,
(*Bring the baby down.*)
Jump over the snow.
(*Move the baby
up and down again.*)

LAUGHING AND HAVING FUN

Open, Shut Them

Open, shut them,
Open, shut them,
Give a little clap.
*(Open and close your fingers
and then clap.)*
Open, shut them,
Open, shut them,
Put them in your lap.
*(Open and close your fingers
and put them in your lap.)*
Creep them, creep them,
Creep them, creep them,
Slowly to your chin.
(Creep up to the baby's chin.)
Open up your little mouth,
But do not let them in.
*(Place your fingers on the baby's lips and then quickly put your arms behind
your back.)*

I'm Gonna Get Your Nose

I'm gonna get your nose,
Yes sir, yes siree.
I'm gonna get your nose,
Yes sir, yes sir, yes siree.
*(Each time you say "nose,"
kiss the baby's nose.)*

I'm gonna get your toes,
Yes sir, yes siree.
I'm gonna get your toes,
Yes sir, yes sir, yes siree.
(Each time you say "toes," kiss the baby's toes.)

I'm gonna get your tummy
(Repeat the verse.)

LAUGHING AND HAVING FUN

Hickory, Dickory, Dare

Hickory, dickory, dare,
A pig flew up in the air.
(Swing the baby high into the air.)
Bobby Brown,
Soon brought him down.
(Bring the baby down into your arms.)
Hickory, dickory, dare.
(Instead of the name, use the baby's name.)

Me

10 little fingers,
10 little toes,
2 little eyes and
1 little nose.
2 little cheeks,
1 little chin and
1 little mouth where the candy goes in!
(Touch the baby's body parts as you say the rhyme.)

LAUGHING AND HAVING FUN

Swing Me Over

Swing me over the water,
Swing me over the sea,
Swing me over the garden wall,
And swing me home for tea.

Swing me over the treetops,
Swing me over the zoo,
Swing me over the garden wall,
And swing me back to you!
(Swing the baby back and forth)

This Is My Right Hand

This is my right hand,
I raise it up high.
This is my left hand,
I reach to the sky.
Right hand, left hand,
Roll them round and round.
Right hand, left hand,
Pound, pound, pound.
(Take the baby's hands and move them accordingly.)

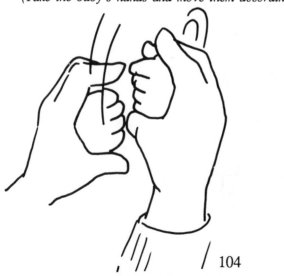

LAUGHING AND HAVING FUN

Father Fell Off

Father, Mother, and Uncle John,
Rode to the doctor one by one,
(Bounce the baby on your knee.)
Father fell off,
(Slide the baby off to the side.)
Mother fell off,
(Slide the baby off to the other side,)
And Uncle John rode on and on.
(Bounce the baby up and down again.)
Father fell off,
Mother fell off,
And Uncle John rode on.
*(Slide and bounce the baby
as you did before.)*

Turkey Turkey

Turkey, turkey,
Wobble, wobble, wobble.
(Move your head back and forth.)
Turkey, turkey,
Gobble, gobble, gobble.
(Nuzzle the baby's nose.)

LAUGHING AND HAVING FUN

See My Fingers

See my fingers dance and play,
Fingers dance for me today.
See my ten toes dance and play,
Ten toes dance for me today.
(Take the baby's hands and feet and move them
 to the rhyme.)

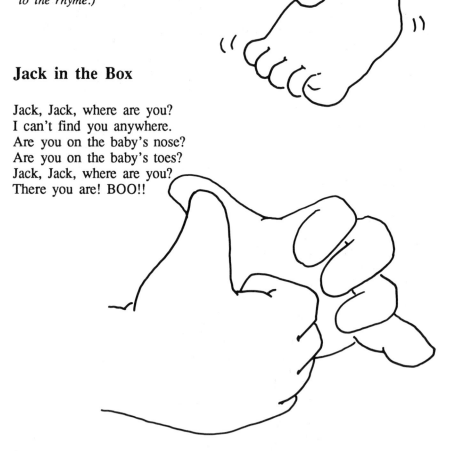

Jack in the Box

Jack, Jack, where are you?
I can't find you anywhere.
Are you on the baby's nose?
Are you on the baby's toes?
Jack, Jack, where are you?
There you are! BOO!!

(Wrap your fingers around your thumb. Touch the baby's nose and toes.
When you come to "BOO." unwrap your fingers and stick out your thumb.)

LAUGHING AND HAVING FUN

Tickley

Tickley, tickley, where should I tickley?
(Sway the baby as you say the chant.)
Tickley, tickley, right on the nose,
(Stop swaying, and tickle the baby on the nose.)
Tickley, tickley, where should I tickley?
(Start swaying again.)
Tickley, tickley, right on the tummy.
(Stop swaying and tickle the baby on the tummy.)

Whoops Johnny!

Johnny, Johnny, Johnny, Johnny,
Whoops! Johhny,
Whoops! Johnny,
Johnny, Johnny,
Johnny.

(Touch each of the baby's fingers on the word "Johnny," starting with the smallest finger. Slide down the index finger and up the thumb on the word "whoops," then slide back down the thumb and up the index finger.)

LAUGHING AND HAVING FUN

Up in the Air

Up in the air we fly, fly, fly,
(*Hold the baby high in the air.*)
Flying in the sky, sky, sky.
Here's a birdie,
Tweet, tweet, tweet,
Here's a cloud to rest your feet.
Now it's time to go back home,
ZOOOOOOOOM!!
(*Bring the baby down
and give her a hug.*)

Little Mouse

There was a little mouse,
Who had a little house,
And he lived way, way up there.
Then he'd creep, creep, creep,
Down through his house,
Into a hole down there.
(*Start tickling the baby's head and work your way down to her toes.*)

ROCKING AND SLEEPING

O Sweetly Does My Baby Sleep

O sweetly does my baby sleep,
When he awakes from slumber deep,
Bright sparking jewels I'll show him,
Gay colored balls I'll throw him.

My baby in his cradle lies,
To him I sing sweet lullabies,
Gently his cradle I'm rocking,
While over him I am watching.

Sleep My Baby

Sleep my baby near to me,
Lu, lu, lu, lu, lu, lu.
Close your velvet eyes.
Far away in their nest,
Baby birds flutter down to rest.
High in the trees,
Far from harm,
Tiny monkey sleeps,
Deep in his mother's arms.
Sleep my baby near to me,
Lu, lu, lu, lu, lu.

ROCKING AND SLEEPING

Hush Little Baby

Hush little baby, don't say a word,
Mama's gonna buy you a mocking bird.
And if that mocking bird won't sing,
Mama's gonna buy you a diamond ring.
And if that diamond ring turns brass,
Mama's gonna buy you a looking glass.
And if that looking glass get's broke,
Mama's gonna buy you a billy goat.
And if that billy goat won't pull,
Mama's gonna buy you a cart and bull.
And if that cart and bull turn over,
Mama's gonna buy you a dog named Rover.
And if that dog named Rover won't bark,
Mama's gonna buy you a horse and cart.
And if that horse and cart fall down,
You'll still be the sweetest little baby in town.

The Man in the Moon

The man in the moon,
Looked out of the moon,
Looked out of the moon and said,
"'Tis time for all of
The children on earth,
To think about going to bed!"
Nighty night,
Nighty night,
Sleep tight,
Nighty night.

ROCKING AND SLEEPING

Baby's Boat

Baby's boat's a silver moon,
Sailing o'er the sky,
Sailing o'er a sea of dreams,
While the clouds roll by.

Sail baby, sail,
Out across the sea,
Only don't forget to sail,
Back again to me.

Baby's fishing for a dream,
Fishing near and far,
His line a silver moonbeam is,
His bait a silver star,

Sail baby, sail,
Out across the sea,
Only don't forget to sail,
Back again to me.

The Bamboo Flute

From the bamboo, mother makes a flute,
Bamboo flute for baby small.
Held in little hands,
Pressed to rosy lips,
Lilting melodies rise and fall,
Lu, lu, lu, lu.
Melodies rise and fall
Lu, lu, lu, lu,
Sleepy heads nod and fall.

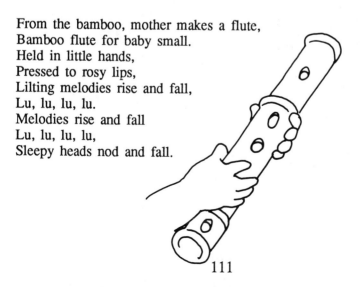

111

ROCKING AND SLEEPING

Wee Willie Winkie

Wee Willie Winkie,
Runs through the town,
Upstairs and downstairs,
In his night gown.
Rapping at the window,
Crying through the locks,
"Are the children in their beds,
For now it's eight o'clock?"

Stretch up High

Stretch up high,
As tall as a house,
(Stretch the baby's hands up high.)
Curl up small,
As small as a mouse.
(Show the baby how to curl up small.)
Now pretend you have a drum,
And beat like this, rum, tum, tum,
(Pretend you are playing a drum.)
Shake your fingers, stamp your feet,
(Do both actions.)
Close your eyes and go to sleep.
(Pretend to go to sleep.)

ROCKING AND SLEEPING

Let's Go to the Woods

"Let's go to the woods,"
Said this little pig.
(Wiggle the baby's left foot.)
"What shall we do there?"
Said this little pig.
(Wiggle the baby's right foot.)
"Look for our mother,"
Said this little pig.
(Wiggle the baby's left arm.)
"What shall we do with mother?"
Said this little pig.
(Wiggle the baby's right arm.)
"Kiss her all over,"
Said this little pig.
(Kiss the baby all over.)

Back and Forth

Back and forth I rock the baby,
Back and forth,
Back and forth.
Go to sleep my precious baby,
I will watch you all the night.

Back and forth I rock the baby,
Back and forth,
Back and forth.
Pleasant dreams my precious baby,
When you wake I'll be right here.

ROCKING AND SLEEPING

Come Let's to Bed

"Come, let's to bed,"
Says Sleepy Head.
"Tarry a while," says Slow.
"Put on the pan,"
Says Greedy Nan,
"We'll sup before we go."

(*Say this rhyme as you rock your baby. Repeat it several times and get slower and slower on each repeat.*)

High in the Deep Blue Sky

High there in the deep blue sky,
Down the Milky Way,
Rides a ship without a sail,
With no oars, they say.
On the ship,
It's only crew
Is a rabbit white.
Westward it floats onward,
Quietly through the night.

ROCKING AND SLEEPING

Ho Ho Watanay

Ho, ho, watanay,
Ho, ho, watanay,
Ho ho watanay,
Ki yokena, ki yokena,
Sleep, sleep,
Little one.
Sleep, sleep little one,
Sleep, sleep,
Little one,
Now go to sleep,
Now go to sleep.

Rock-A-Bye Baby

Rock-a-bye baby,
In the tree tops,
When the wind blows,
The cradle will rock.
When the bough breaks,
The cradle will fall,
Down will come baby,
Cradle and all.

Rock-a-bye baby,
Thy cradle is green,
Daddy's a nobleman,
Mommy's a queen.
Betty's a lady,
And wears a gold ring,
Johnny's a drummer,
And drums for the king.

ROCKING AND SLEEPING

Go to Bed Late

Go to bed late,
Stay very small.
Go to bed early,
Grow very tall.

Go to bed first,
A golden purse.
Go to bed second,
A golden pheasant.
Go to bed third,
A golden bird.
Go to bed fourth,
A golden horse.
Go to bed fifth,
A golden kiss.
(Kiss the baby on the cheek.)

I See the Moon

I see the moon,
And the moon sees me,
God bless the moon,
And God bless me.

I see the stars,
And the stars see me,
God bless the stars,
And God bless me.

ROCKING AND SLEEPING

Blowing Wind

The wind, the wind,
Is passing through
Rustling leaves,
Whispering to the trees.

I'm the west wind,
I bring the summer rain,
When I blow softly,
I whisper your name.
*(Blow gently on the baby's forehead
and whisper the baby's name.)*

Good Night

Good night, sweet baby,
Good night, sweet one,
The clock is ticking,
And says "we're done."

Good night, sweet baby,
Good night, my dear,
The stars are twinkling,
And sleep is near.

Good night, sleep tight,
Don't let the bedbugs bite.

ROCKING AND SLEEPING

Bedtime for Piggies

"It's time for piggies to go to bed,"
Mother piggie said.
"I will count them up to see,
If all of my piggies came back to me.
One little piggy, two little piggies,
Three little piggies, dear.
Four little piggies, five little piggies,
Yes, they all are here.
You are the dearest little piggies alive,
One, two, three, four, five."
(Count the baby's toes.)

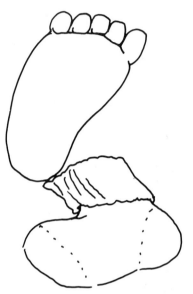

Baby Talk

Little baby, little baby,
How were you today?
Were you hot or were you cold,
What do you have to say?
Goo, goo, goo, goo,
Ga, ga, ga.

Little baby, little baby,
What did you do today?
Did you smile, did you laugh,
What do you have to say?
Goo, goo, goo, goo,
Ga, ga, ga.
*(Rock the baby as
you say the baby talk.)*

ROCKING AND SLEEPING

Candles

Little Nancy Netticoat
Wears a white petticoat.
The longer she lives
The shorter she grows.
Little Nancy Netticoat.

Sleep my little baby
While the candle burns.
Sleep my little baby
While the candle burns.

Old Woman

There was an old woman,
Tossed high in a basket,
Seventeen times as high as the moon,
Where she was going,
I couldn't but ask it,
For in her hand she carried a broom.
"Old woman, old woman, old woman." said I,
"Where are you going to up so high?"
"To brush the cobwebs off the sky!"
"May I go with you?"
"Aye, by and by."

ROCKING AND SLEEPING

Baby-O

What shall I do with the baby-o?
What shall I do with the baby-o?
What shall I do with the baby-o?,
Time to go to sleep.

I will rock the baby-o,
I will rock the baby-o,
I will rock the baby-o,
Time to go to sleep.

I will kiss the baby-o,
I will kiss the baby-o,
I will kiss the baby-o,
Time to go to sleep.
(Do the actions as you chant the rhyme.)

Let's Go to Bed

Come let's go to bed, bed,
Come let's go to bed.
Rest your sleepy head, head,
Come let's go to bed.

Close your pretty eyes, eyes,
Close your pretty eyes.
Rest your sleepy head, head,
Close your pretty eyes.

ROCKING AND SLEEPING

Irene, Goodnight

Irene, good night, Irene,
Irene, good night,
Good night, Irene,
Good night, Irene,
I'll see you in my dreams.
(Substitute the baby's name for "Irene.")

Rock-A-My-Soul

Rock-a-my soul in the bosom of Abraham,
Rock-a-my soul in the bosom of Abraham,
Rock-a-my soul in the bosom of Abraham,
Oh, rock-a-my soul.
(Rock the baby back and forth.)

So high, you can't get over it.
(Rock the baby to one side and hold.)
So low, you can't get under it.
(Rock baby to the other side and hold.)
So wide, you can't get around it.
(Rock baby back and forth.)
Oh, rock-a-my soul.
(Repeat the first verse.)

GUIDELINES FOR GROWTH

ZERO TO SIX MONTHS

Motor, Auditory and Visual Skills

Holds up head
Grasps a rattle or toy
Rolls from back to side
Sits with hand support
Pulls to sitting position holding adult fingers
Follows moving objects with eyes
Focuses eyes on small objects
Begins to reach for objects

Picks up block
Transfers objects from hand to hand
Reacts with a startle to a noise
Turns head in direction of a bell
Turns head toward voice sound
Responds to voices with an activity

Language and Cognitive Skills

Babbles and coos
Gurgles on seeing others
Makes simple sounds
Repeats same sound
Smiles, chuckles, laughs
Attempts a variety of sounds
Smiles in response to attention

Shows eagerness by making sounds
Fusses when a favorite toy is removed
Reacts to the sight of a toy
Attempts to repeat things enjoyed before

Self Concept Skills

Inspects own hands
Brings things to mouth
Focuses eyes on own moving hands
Smiles at mirror image
Vocalizes at mirror image

Anticipates feeding
Plays unattended for 10 minutes
Picks up spoon
Feeds self a cracker
Holds a bottle part of the time

Lifts cup with handle
Looks directly at a person's face
Recognizes a parent
Reaches for familiar persons

Responds to "Peek-a-Boo"
Smiles in response to facial expressions

SIX TO TWELVE MONTHS

Motor, Auditory and Visual Skills

Bounces when held in a standing position
Sits unsupported
Pulls pegs from a pegboard
Rolls a ball while sitting
Crawls rapidly, climbs on stairs
Stands unaided
Moves hand to follow eye focus
Picks up small objects with thumb and finger
Bangs two blocks together

Looks at pictures in books
Drops small objects into containers
Responds to voice tones and inflections
Recognizes familiar words and responds accordingly
Shakes bell in imitation of an adult
Stops activity after hearing "No"
Shows interest in certain words and gestures

Language and Cognitive Skills

Imitates speech sounds
Babbles rhythmically
Combines two syllables
Imitates sounds of dogs, clocks, cows, etc.
Expresses first real words other than "mama" and "dada"
Attracts attention by making noises
Imitates clapping hands
Waves "bye-bye"
Follows simple directions
Understands "No"

Shakes head to indicate "No"
Pulls string to obtain a toy
Finds block hidden under a cup
Knows meaning of "Mama" and "Dada"
Removes a block from a cup when shown
Squeezes a toy to make it squeak
Looks to find toys which have disappeared from sight.

Self Concept Skills

Seeks or demands attention
Pushes away another's hands to keep a toy
Holds arms in front of face to avoid being washed

Able to finger feed self
Drinks from cup with help
Controls drooling
Responds to another's gestures
Plays "Patty Cake"

Holds arms out to be picked up
Sucks soft foods from spoon
Holds, bites, chews a cracker

Repeats a performance when laughed at
Cooperates when dressing by holding arms out

TWELVE TO TWENTY-FOUR MONTHS

Motor, Auditory and Visual Skills

Baby walks independently
Holds two small objects in one hand
Walks up and down stairs with help
Jumps in place
Kicks large ball
Throws small ball overhand
Recognizes familiar person
Scribbles on paper
Stacks three to six blocks
Turns knobs

Can find objects of the same color, shape or size
Points to distant interesting objects outdoors
Turns toward a family member whose name is spoken
Understands and follows a simple command
Notices sounds like the sound of a clock, bell, or whistle
Responds rhythmically to music
Carries out two-step directions

Language and Cognitive Skills

Jabbers with expression
Identifies with pictures in books
Uses single words meaningfully

Names objects when asked, "What's this?"
Uses twenty or more words

Names twenty-five familiar objects
Gestures to make wants known
Names toys
Uses words to make wants known
Combines two different words
Tries to sing
Speaks in simple sentences

Finds familiar objects
Imitates fitting objects into containers
Turns two or three pages of a book at a time
Points to named pictures in a book
Remembers where an object belongs
Uses a stick or string

Self Concept Skills

Demands personal attention
Points to three named body parts
Insists on helping to feed self
Names body parts on a doll
Claims objects as her own
Refers to self by name
Pulls off socks
Eats with a spoon
Drinks from a cup

Attempts washing self
Offers toy but does not release it
Plays independently around another child
Helps parents with simple tasks
Plays contentedly alone if near adults
Enjoys short walks
Asks for food and water when needed

INDEX OF FIRST LINES

MISS JACKIE MUSIC COMPANY

BOOKS

GREAT BIG BOOK OF RHYTHM
144 pages of ideas using rhythm to teach listening, language, motor and cognitive skills, and to strengthen self-concept. $12.95

SNIGGLES, SQUIRRELS AND CHICKEN POX
40 delightful original songs with words, music and chords, plus activities introduced by *Miss Jackie* in the *Instructor* magazine. $8.95

SONGS TO SING WITH BABIES
Songs, games and activities for rocking and nursing, cuddling, waking up and dressing baby. $8.95

GAMES TO PLAY WITH BABIES
Over 100 delightful games for babies from birth through two years of age. Learning games, laughing games, bath games and more. $8.95

MY TOES ARE STARTING TO WIGGLE
108 songs with activities for circle time all year long. 196 pages full of developmentally appropriate teaching ideas and flannel board patterns. $12.95

PEANUT BUTTER, TARZAN AND ROOSTERS
Language and movement activities, flannel board patterns, bulletin board ideas and art activities to go with the recoring of the same name. $8.95

LOLLIPOPS AND SPAGHETTI
Dozens of teacher-tested ideas to develop skills. Companion to the best-selling cassette of the same name. $8.95

THE ULTIMATE EARLY CHILDHOOD MUSIC RESOURCE BOOK..OPUS 1
Songs and activities for every month of the year. Includes learning center, circle time, infants and toddler activities and music reviews. Everything you ever wanted to know about music for young children. $19,95

THE ULTIMATE EARLY CHILDHOOD MUSIC RESOURCE...OPUS 2
Just like Opus 1 but with all new and innovative songs and activities. $19.95

BUMP, THUMP, RATTLE, BOO!: A CAULDRON OF MUSICAL TREATS FOR HALLOWEEN.

Songs, poems, chants, rhymes, musical plays, Halloween safety and movement activities. A unique resource for young children. $9.95

RECORDS AND TAPES

LOLLIPOPS AND SPAGHETTI *(Recorded live)*

Valuable learning is mixed with songs that are fun to sing and hear, including "The Lollipop Tree" and "On Top of Spaghetti." Cassette only. $9.95

PEANUT BUTTER, TARZAN AND ROOSTERS *(Recorded live)*

"Peanut Butter," "I'm So Mad I Could Scream," and many more songs that teach important fundamentals such as self concept and fun. $9.95

SNIGGLES, SQUIRRELS AND CHICKENPOX, VOL.1

24 track album includes "Baby Bear's Chickenpox," and many other seasonal songs in a variety of moods and tempos. $9.95

SNIGGLES, SQUIRRELS AND CHICKENPOX, VOL.2

Charming songs in many styles of music with wonderful sound effects and a variety of instruments and voices. Includes "Sing About Martin," "Ride Sally Ride," and many more. $9.95

SING AROUND THE WORLD *(Recorded live)*

A wonderful multi-cultural experience with children learning and singing songs from several countries. The participation is vigorous. $9.95

HELLO RHYTHM

Self directed rhythm songs that children can do with Miss Jackie. "All The Fish," "Miss Mary Mac," and many other participatory songs. $9.95

SONGS TO SING WITH BABIES *(Cassette only)*

Songs from the book of the same name. Recorded in the order they appear in the book so that adults can learn them and babies can listen. $8.95

GAMES TO PLAY WITH BABIES *(Cassette only)*

A book on tape. Two cassettes read by Drew Dimmel, famous radio personality. 0-1 year and 1-2 years. $9.95 for each tape.

SING A JEWISH SONG *(Recorded live)*
Recorded in St. Louis with hundreds of parents and children singing, laughing and actively participating in the music. $9.95

VIDEOS

BABY BEAR'S CHICKEN POX PLUS 15 MORE BLOCKBUSTER HITS BY "MISS JACKIE"
The kids at Scott Kindergarten *LOVE* music by "Miss Jackie". They made up dances and plays, put on costumes and sang their hearts out to two video cameras. Great fun to watch. VHS only. $16.95

MISS JACKIE LIVE
Miss Jackie visited a kindergarten in Michigan and the school district taped her performance. Children enjoy singing and acting out many of her famous songs. VHS only. $16.95

ABOUT MISS JACKIE

Better known as "Miss Jackie" to thousands of teachers, parents and children throughout the United States and Canada, Jackie Weissman is a children's concert artist, author, composer, educator, consultant, national columnist, recording artist and television personality.

An adjunct instructor in Early Childhood Education at Emporia (Kansas) State University and Music Reviewer plus a monthly columnist for "The Instructor Magazine."

Jackie Weissman has written many books dealing with music, rhythm games and young children. She has also produced many recordings (mostly her own songs) and workshops - on both audio and video tape - which are widely used for teacher training.

Music by "Miss Jackie" appears in college texts, most elementary music books and learning kits for language, math and social studies. She has written music for The Campbell Soup Co., The Kellogg Co., The American Royal and most recently for "Worlds of Fun", a theme park that is using Miss Jackie's songs for the themes in their shows. Children perform her music throughout the world.

A frequent keynote speaker and workshop presenter as well as a concert presenter for children and their parents, "Miss Jackie" has inspired hundreds of thousands of parents, teachers, and children.

For a free catalog, please write:

MISS JACKIE MUSIC COMPANY
10001 EL MONTE
OVERLAND PARK, KANSAS 66207
(913) 381-3672

ADD YOUR OWN RHYMES

ADD YOUR OWN RHYMES

ADD YOUR OWN RHYMES

ADD YOUR OWN RHYMES

5179